Two Little Girls and the Special Book

Once in time and far away...

Once in time and far away
a place called Forest Rock
Where little people and their kids
would strangely smile a lot!

No one knew exactly
what would cause them all to say
"The Lord is good and we are blessed
for we all love to pray"

Two little girls adventure called
a treasure to be found
All they must do is seek the Truth
that leaves them both astound

Mommy's special plan

There once were girls, twins they could be

their ages two and four

They'd play with simple toys and sing

but sometimes it's a bore

Their mommy had a plan

to teach them of the greater good

A special gift to hide and seek

the toy box they must look

To ten they'd count to run and see
what's hidden in the box
A special book with words that bring
excitement, joy and shock!

They opened up the book
and saw the pages glowing white
To learn about the Father
and His Power, Strength and Might!

The girls then read a verse aloud
their hearts felt nice and warm
It spoke about the Son of God
of Jesus, King of All!

Let's learn about His Truth and Love
and trust with all our hearts
The guidance of the Holy Ghost
and He will light your paths

Londyn hears
the Word

Our little girl named Londyn-Skye
found favor in the Lord
She prayed one day with palms upright
"is this Lord why I'm called?

To pray the lame and sick away
in people wrapped with cords?
With worship in the Holy Ghost
the healed are left in awe

Your Power and your Mighty Strength
will set all captives free
And all it takes are prayers in faith
and love from You and me"

The Lord heard every word she said
and spoke into her ear
"My Word is true and never fails
and ends all pain and fear

I'll be with you both night and day
and as you pray I'll call
The things unseen into this world
from Heaven's open door

Then Londyn-Skye jumped to her feet
and sang and worshiped God
With songs in Spirit and in truth
'cause Jesus heard her heart

This story told the walk-by-faith
of Londyn since she crawled
To where she walks and talks and sings
in honor of the Lord

Bella says
NO
to fear

The school bell rang and Bella
felt some fear inside her heart
That scary day has come you see
from mommy she must part

Her mommy took her by the hand
and walked her to the door
And said to Bella "do not fear,
your help comes from the Lord"

Then Bella smiled and waved goodbye
of Scripture she then thought
That Power, Love, a Mind so Sound...
it all comes from the Lord!

The fear she had then went away
as courage filled her heart
"All things I can do in His name,
this journey I will start"

Let's see how Bella makes new friends
as fear has now been fought
By simply having trust and faith
in Jesus, our sweet Lord

Little
Johnny

Little Johnny was a boy
a troubled start to life
With orange hair and freckled cheeks
his heart would long to strife

Now Johnny hid behind his mask
an angry face he wore
As kids would always point and laugh
his heart felt really sore

"A little friend I long to have
I wish this shame will stop
For every time a finger points
and calls me Carrot Top!"

But Bella saw his broken heart
and walked across the floor
She said to Johnny "dry your tears
for Jesus knows you more!

Johnny heard the kindness
and the love in Bellla's voice
"You are perfect in His eyes
for you were made by choice"

Every day from that day on
they both would laugh and play
For Johnny made a special friend
his masks - all thrown away

A little

goes a

long way

Londyn and her sister smelled
the bread from far away
Their daddy walked behind them
to accompany and pay

As Londyn neared the entrance to
ol Dan the baker's shop
She noticed sadness from a man
who's tummy rumbled lots

No money did he have to buy
a bread or juice to drink
For all he had were clothes to wear
and shoes that made him itch!

A little board he held to ask
the people for some help
Some food to feed him and to stop
the way his tummy felt

Then Londyn thought of how you feed
the poor by giving bread
The Lord repays your deeds
for when you give, to Him you lend

The man's eyes filled with water as
he felt what once was lost
For such a small act from the heart
restored his faith in God

"if you confess with your

mouth the Lord Jesus and

believe in your heart that God

has raised Him from the dead,

you will be saved."

Romans 10:9

The end

Made in the USA
Middletown, DE
09 February 2023

24408303R00029